MERCER MAYER'S

LC + THE CRITTER KIDS

MYSTERY AT BIG HORN RANCH

A Golden Book • New York

Western Publishing Company, Inc., Racine, Wisconsin 53404

A Mercer Mayer Ltd./J. R. Sansevere Book

Library of Congress Catalog Card Number: 94-73090
ISBN: 0-307-15978-7/ISBN: 0-307-65978-X (lib. bdg.)   A MCMXCV

Written by Erica Farber/J. R. Sansevere

LC

VELVET

LITTLE SISTE

TIGER

KOOL BEAR

SLICK RICK

SU SU   GABBY   TIMOTHY

GATOR   FLEX   HENRIETTA

CHAPTER 1

CITY SLICKERS

"Are we there yet?" asked LC, taking off his headphones.

"Almost," said Mr. Hogwash, the Critter Kids' teacher. "The ranch should be just over that hill."

"Cool," said Tiger, LC's best friend. "Hey, LC, can I listen to your new Red Hot Chili Critters tape?"

"Just don't press the blue button," said LC, handing his Walkman to Tiger. "It's for recording. The PLAY button is green."

"Okay," said Tiger, putting on the headphones.

"I can't wait to ride a horse," said Gabby. She tapped the toes of her new cowboy boots against the floor.

"I can't wait to sleep under the stars," said Velvet.

"I can't wait to get some grub," said Henrietta, popping her last chocolate cookie in her mouth. "I'm starved."

"And I can't wait to rope some cattle," said LC, twirling his rope.

Just then Mr. Hogwash slammed on the brakes. The bus screeched to a stop. Right in the middle of the road was a cow!

Mr. Hogwash beeped the horn. The cow didn't move. He beeped again. The cow still didn't move.

"Hey, LC, here's your big chance to rope some cattle," said Su Su.

"No problem," said LC.

Mr. Hogwash opened the door. LC and

the Critter Kids got off the bus.

"Well?" demanded Su Su, pointing her riding crop in LC's face.

"Chill," said Tiger. "Give the dude a chance to get set."

LC began to uncoil his rope. He tried hard not to look at the cow's horns. They were really big and sharp.

"All we have to do is get the lasso over the cow's head and then we can just pull him off the road," said LC.

"Cool," said Gator.

LC held the rope over his head and started to swing it around. The cow stared at him.

"Will you just do it?" said Gabby.

LC closed his eyes and threw the rope. Everybody started to laugh.

"A-hem," said Mr. Hogwash, clearing his throat, "Mr. Critter."

LC opened his eyes. He couldn't believe it. He'd missed the cow and lassoed Mr. Hogwash instead.

"I don't think you know what you're doing at all," said Su Su.

"Give me that rope," said Gabby.

Suddenly a horse came galloping over the hill. The rider was swinging a rope

high in the air. In a second the rider let go of the rope. It sailed perfectly over the cow's horns and landed right around its neck. The rider jerked the rope and pulled the cow to the side of the road.

"Awesome!" exclaimed Tiger.

The rider jumped off the horse and walked over to the Critter Kids.

"Cool riding, cowboy," said LC.

The cowboy took off his hat and shook out a mane of long blond hair.

"You're a girl!" said LC, his eyes wide.

"Missy's the name," the girl said. "My daddy owns the Big Horn Dude Ranch."

"Oh," said LC.

"You must be those city slickers," said Missy.

"What exactly do you mean by city slickers?" asked Timothy. "Actually, we don't come from the city at all. We're from Critterville."

"You're city slickers just the same," said Missy. "And you don't know nothin' 'bout a ranch like ropin' and ridin' and stuff like that."

"Excuse me," said Su Su, smoothing a wrinkle out of her jodhpurs. "I happen to know how to ride. In fact, I just won a blue ribbon in a horse show last week."

Missy started to laugh. "That's not ridin', that's showin'," said Missy. "These here horses ain't show horses. They're wild broncos. And you gotta be real tough to ride 'em."

"Well, I'm tough," said LC.

"Yeah," said Tiger. "He's tough."

"Yeah, right," said Missy, looking LC up and down.

Just then a red pickup truck came speeding down the road and squealed its tires to a stop in front of them. A tall cowboy got out of the cab.

"Sorry 'bout that cow, Missy," said the cowboy. "We keep tryin' to fix those fences, but the cattle break 'em down faster than we can fix 'em."

Missy stared at the cowboy. "If we lose one more cow we lose the ranch," she said. With that, she hopped back on her horse and trotted away with the cow in tow.

"I wonder what she means by that," said Gabby.

"From what I've read," said Timothy, "prize heifers can be worth $100,000 or more."

"Wow!" said LC. "I didn't know cows could cost so much."

"Welcome to Big Horn Dude Ranch," said the cowboy, turning to Mr. Hogwash and the Critter Kids. "Sorry for all the trouble. Slim's the name. I'm trail master of the ranch and I'll be showin' you 'round."

"Nice to meet you," said Mr. Hogwash.

"Follow me," said Slim. "The ranch is just a piece up this road."

The Critter Kids got back on the bus and headed for Big Horn Dude Ranch.

CHAPTER 2

THE DISAPPEARING COWS

"This here is Cabin A, where you gals will sleep tomorrow night," said Slim. "And over there beyond those trees is Cabin B, where you fellas will sleep."

"So these are real log cabins," said LC.

"That's right," said Slim. "They were built over one hundred years ago by Mr. Big Horn's ancestors when they first settled in these here parts."

"Wow!" said Gabby. "I've never slept in an historic landmark before."

"What's that little house over there?"

asked Henrietta, pointing to a small wooden shack behind the cabins.

"That's the outhouse," said Slim.

"Outhouse?" repeated Su Su, raising her eyebrows.

"Yep," said Slim. "These cabins don't have any modern plumbin', so when nature calls, you have to go out—to the outhouse."

"No plumbing?" said Su Su. "You mean there's no bathroom in our cabin?"

"Nope," said Slim, shaking his head.

"That's what the outhouse is for," said Henrietta.

"That's disgusting," said Su Su. "There's electricity, right?"

"Nope," said Slim, shaking his head again.

"Then how am I going to plug in my blow dryer?" asked Su Su.

"Give me a break," said Gabby. "This is the Wild West."

Suddenly a loud clanging noise rang out.

"What's that?" asked Velvet.

"That's the breakfast bell," said Slim. "It's chow time."

Slim and the Critter Kids were the last to arrive at the Big Horn mess hall. They sat down on two benches on either side of a long wooden table.

"Welcome to Big Horn Dude Ranch," said a fat critter at the head of the table. "I'm Mr. Big Horn," he added with a wide smile. "It's chow time. So dig in, kids. I want to see those plates clean as a whistle."

"Why do we have to clean our plates?" asked Gator. "Aren't we here to eat?"

"It's just a saying," explained Timothy. "It means to eat everything on your plate."

"What's this stuff?" asked LC, picking up

one of the bowls on the table.

"Oatmeal, I guess," said Tiger.

"No, I believe they're grits," said Timothy. "They're a popular western breakfast item, if I recall."

LC took a big spoonful and passed the bowl to Gator. "What are grits made of?" asked LC, chewing on a mouthful.

"Cow innards and calf brains," said Missy with a smirk.

LC's eyes opened wide. He grabbed his napkin and spit out the grits.

"Gross," said Su Su. "I'm not touching that stuff."

"Grits are actually just ground-up corn," said Timothy.

LC looked at Missy.

"I'm just kidding, tough guy," said Missy.

"I don't care what they're made of," said Henrietta. "I think they're yummy."

"Listen up, everybody," Slim said, tapping his spoon against his glass. "When you're done eatin', I'm gonna fix ya up on some horses and we're gonna go on a nice long ride and camp out under the stars."

All the Critter Kids cheered.

Just then the door to the mess hall burst open and the sheriff strode in with his deputy right behind him.

"Mornin' Sheriff Buckeye, Deputy Doodle," said Mr. Big Horn. "Any news?"

"I hate to barge in like this," said Sheriff Buckeye, "but Deputy Doodle and I did a complete search of your property yesterday afternoon. We didn't find hide nor hair of your missing cow."

"And no trace of the other two either," added Deputy Doodle.

"I just don't understand how my three most valuable cows could vanish like that," said Mr. Big Horn with a sigh.

"Well," said the sheriff, "the only clue we did find was another set of cattle hoofprints leading into the corral at the old Ghost Valley ranch."

"I think the ghost got them there cows," said Deputy Doodle.

"Quiet, Doodle!" barked Sheriff Buckeye. "Mr. Big Horn don't believe in ghosts, or he wouldn't have bought the old Ghost Valley ranch in the first place."

"I don't know what to believe anymore," said Mr. Big Horn, shaking his head. "All I do know is that until I started ranchin' on that land, I wasn't missing any cattle. If things continue like this, I'm gonna have no choice but to close the ranch." He turned to the Critter Kids. "If you'll excuse me," he said.

Sheriff Buckeye and Deputy Doodle followed Mr. Big Horn out of the room.

"Wow!" said Gabby. "A ghost."

"Ooooh," said Velvet. "It sounds scary."

"So, Missy," began Gabby, turning to Missy.

"She's gone," said Su Su.

"How weird," said Gabby, looking around the table. "Something strange is going on around here."

"Maybe," said LC. "But it doesn't have

anything to do with us."

"In fact," continued Gabby, ignoring LC, "it sounds like a perfect case for the Critter Kids Detective Club."

Uh-oh, thought LC. Here we go again . . .

CHAPTER 3

RIDE 'EM COWBOY!

After breakfast LC and the Critter Kids followed Slim out to the corral.

"All right, dudes," said Slim. "It's time to cowboy up."

"Cool," said LC. "I can't wait to ride."

"Will you forget about horses for a minute," said Gabby. "We've got to find out more about this ghost."

"No, we don't," said LC. "It's got nothing to do with us."

Slim led a large chestnut mare out of the stable. "Here's a real beaut for you, Su Su," said Slim. "Her name's Honey."

"Thank you," Su Su said, smoothly mounting onto the horse's back.

"I hope ya don't mess up yer clothes," said Slim, looking from Su Su's shiny leather riding boots all the way up to her black velvet hard hat. "I mean, they're pretty fancy for trail ridin'."

"Actually, they're for dressage," said Su Su. "I couldn't possibly ride wearing anything else."

Slim just chuckled. "And here's your horse," he said, leading a dappled gray over to Gabby. "His name's Tall Freddy."

Slim helped Gabby put her foot in the stirrup and swing onto the horse. Tall Freddy stood there, calmly munching on some grass.

"Hey, Slim," Missy called from her perch on the corral fence. "Make sure you give that tough guy over there the Appaloosa," she said, pointing to LC.

Slim shook his head. "I don't know if that's such a good idea," he said. "I mean, that's just about the wildest darn horse I ever laid eyes on."

"That's okay," said Missy, grinning. "He told me he's tough."

"Are you sure you want to ride that Appaloosa, son?" Slim asked LC.

"Uh . . ." began LC.

"What's the matter, tough guy?" said Missy. "Are you chicken?"

LC gulped. He'd never heard of an Appaloosa before, but even the name sounded a little scary.

"LC's not chicken," said Tiger, patting LC on the back. "This dude is tough."

Slim shrugged his shoulders and went back into the barn.

"Oh, no," whispered LC to Tiger. "What am I gonna do now?"

Before Tiger could answer, Slim led out a huge brown stallion that had lots of white and brown spots. The horse took one look at the Critter Kids and began to buck wildly.

"Whoa, boy!" said Slim, pulling on the horse's reins. "Whoa!"

But the horse wouldn't listen. He kept bucking. Slim tried to rein him in, but the horse kept bucking and bumped into Honey and Su Su. Honey whinnied loudly and reared her front legs.

"Help! Help!" Su Su screamed. A second later Su Su slid off Honey's back and landed right in a mud puddle. The Critter Kids stared at Su Su in shock.

"Are you okay?" asked Velvet.

"I'm fine," said Su Su, standing up and wiping mud off her jodhpurs.

"That was totally wild!" said Tiger.

"Don't tell me LC is riding that monster," said Gabby. "He doesn't even know how to ride."

Finally Slim calmed the horse down. "This here is Buckaroo Bonzai," said Slim, turning to LC. "He's the horse you'll be ridin' today."

"Me?" said LC, gulping.

"Ready, tough guy?" challenged Missy, staring LC right in the eye.

"This dude was born ready," said Tiger, pushing LC toward the horse.

LC's eyes opened wide. He stared from Slim to Buckaroo Bonzai. LC knew that everybody was looking at him. He had no choice. He had to do it.

LC approached Buckaroo Bonzai. "Hi," he said softly, staring into the horse's big brown eyes.

Buckaroo's nostrils flared and he whinnied. LC jumped back.

"What's the matter?" asked Missy, jumping off the corral fence and walking up to LC. "Are you scared?"

LC started getting mad. Before he could

think about it another second, LC marched right up to Buckaroo Bonzai. He put one foot in the stirrup and threw himself across Buckaroo Bonzai's back. He didn't even have time to grab the reins before Buckaroo took off at a gallop around the corral.

"Wow!" said Tiger.

The Critter Kids watched Buckaroo Bonzai gallop and buck his way around the corral with LC stuck to his back like glue.

"Amazing," said Timothy. "I didn't know LC could ride like that."

"Neither did I," said Gabby.

"He's not even holding the reins!" said Missy in amazement.

LC wanted to get off Buckaroo Bonzai more than anything else in the world. But his belt buckle had gotten caught on the saddle and he couldn't get it loose.

"Whoa, boy!" yelled LC. He felt like he was going to throw up. But Buckaroo Bonzai kept right on bucking.

After a few more minutes Buckaroo Bonzai slowed down to a trot and then to a walk. LC was finally able to unhook himself and sit up. "Howdy," said LC with a big grin on his face.

"Well, I'll be gosh darned," said Slim. "I reckon you done broke in that high roller."

The Critter Kids clapped. Even Missy smiled.

"Mighty fine ridin', tough guy," said Missy.

"Mighty fine horse," said LC as he patted Buckaroo.

The rest of the Critter Kids and Mr. Hogwash saddled up. Then Slim led everybody out of the corral. "I think we're ready to go," he said.

"Okeydokey," said Mr. Hogwash, pulling on the reins of a small brown mare.

"Let's move on out, cowboys," said Slim. "We've got a ways to go through the desert before we get to Ghost Valley." He began to trot away from the ranch.

"Ghost Valley!" said Gabby to LC. "That's where the sheriff and the deputy said the cattle were taken. And then they disappeared. It's a perfect chance for us to investigate."

"I don't know if that's such a good idea," said LC. But Gabby didn't hear him. She had already kicked into Tall Freddy's sides and was on her way to Ghost Valley.

CHAPTER 4

GHOST VALLEY

The sun beat down. The desert was the hottest place LC had ever been. "I'm thirsty," LC said.

"Now, everyone, just take one swig of water," said Slim as he stopped his horse by the side of the trail. "You gotta make that water last till we get to Ghost Valley."

LC took a sip of water. It tasted so good. He had to take just one more sip. And then one more. Before he knew it, his canteen was empty.

"Hey, Gabby," said LC, coming up

behind her. "You got any extra water?"

"No," she said as she tilted her canteen and poured the rest of the water over her head. "I'm so hot."

"Me too," said Tiger, wiping the sweat off his forehead.

"I'm having heatstroke," announced Su Su. "I'm going to faint."

"Can I have your water then?" asked Henrietta.

"Shut up!" said Su Su.

"Once we get up those hills," said Slim, "we'll be out of the desert and Ghost Valley will be right below us."

Everyone inched their horses up the last slope. When they got to the top, they could see the whole valley spread out below them. There were cattle grazing on the green grass. And right in the middle of the valley was a burnt-out house. The only thing left standing was a chimney and a broken-down fence.

"Who used to live there?" asked Gabby.

"Well, it's a long story," began Slim, "and I'll tell you all about it when we get down

to the valley." Slim urged his horse on and led the way down into Ghost Valley.

As soon as everybody reached the fence, Slim told them to form a circle with their horses. Missy rolled her eyes and turned her horse around.

"Where are you going?" asked LC. He took off his headphones and hung them from his belt loop.

"I've already heard this story," said Missy. "And I think it's bogus." She rode to the other side of the fence.

Slim moved his horse into the middle of the Critter Kids' circle. Everybody's eyes were on him. "It all began a long time ago, even before Mr. Big Horn's great-great-great-great-granddaddy settled down in this here county," said Slim, chewing on a big wad of tobacco. "There was an old rancher who lived out here all by himself."

"By himself?" asked Velvet.

"That's right," said Slim. "He didn't have any family and he didn't have any friends. All he had was a dog and cattle."

"That's weird," said Su Su.

"Late one night after the rancher had rounded up all his cattle into this here corral, he heard a straaaaange sound," continued Slim.

"What was it?" asked LC.

"It was the most famous outlaw in all of the Wild

West," said Slim, spitting. "They called him Critter the Kid."

"Wow!" said Tiger.

"Critter the Kid and his posse came galloping up to the rancher's house," Slim continued. "And they began to rustle his cattle."

"Rustle?" said Gator. "What does that mean?"

"To steal cattle," explained Timothy.

"Then what happened?" asked Gabby.

"Well, the rancher grabbed his shotgun and started to open the door," said Slim. "And before the door was even halfway open, Critter the Kid twirled his six-shooter and shot the rancher right through the heart."

"Ahhh!" gasped the Critter Kids.

"That's horrible," said Su Su.

"Well, as that old rancher lay there dyin'," continued Slim, "these are the words he said: 'I put a curse on this valley and no one will ever be able to ranch here ever again. My ghost will come back and ruin anybody who tries.'"

"So you believe that the ghost took Mr. Big Horn's missing cattle?" Timothy asked.

"Maybe," said Slim. "Maybe not. But if you look over there, you can see with your very own eyes the tracks of the cow that disappeared last night."

"Ohmygosh!" said Gabby, staring at the ground.

"As you can see, the tracks stop right here," said Slim, spitting some tobacco juice onto the ground where the hoofprints ended. "That's where the ghost must have gotten 'em. And that, cowpokes, is why this is called Ghost Valley."

Just then the corral door banged open against the fence post. Then it slowly squeaked shut. All the Critter Kids stared at the gate as it banged open once 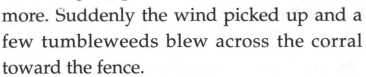 more. Suddenly the wind picked up and a few tumbleweeds blew across the corral toward the fence.

"Looks like we may be in for a little duster," Slim said, squinting his eyes. "It's time to move along. We'll be camping just down the way, over there by Big Oak." He pointed to a large tree about a hundred yards to the right.

"I'm so thirsty," moaned LC.

"Anybody who needs water can fill up their canteens down by the creek, on the other side of the ranch," said Slim.

"I need water," announced Gabby.

"Me too," said LC.

"Me three," added Tiger.

"I'll come along, too," said Timothy.

"Meet us at Big Oak," said Slim. "And don't lollygag by the creek. You don't want to get stuck in a dust storm."

LC, Gabby, Tiger, and Timothy turned their horses around and rode away. They found the creek right where Slim said it would be. LC threw himself down on his stomach and began to drink water in big handfuls right out of the creek.

"This is the best water I ever had," said LC.

Gabby filled up her canteen and poured the water over her head.

"I have a great idea," said Tiger. "Let's go

swimming." He took off his sneakers and did a back flip into the water.

"But Slim said we were supposed to come right back," said Timothy.

"No sweat," said Tiger, shaking water out of his ears. "It'll only take a minute. And Slim said Big Oak isn't very far."

"What about the dust storm?" asked Gabby as the tree branches creaked in the wind.

"Quit worrying," said LC, jumping in after Tiger. "What can a little dust do anyway?"

Just then there was a huge gust of wind. The trees creaked even more. Suddenly a huge branch cracked off a tree and fell into the water. The horses began to spook.

"Uh-oh," said LC. "We better get out of here."

LC and Tiger climbed up onto the bank. Dust was swirling all around them.

"I can't see my shoes," said LC. In fact, the dust was so thick he couldn't even see his own hands in front of him.

"Your shoes are over here," called Gabby.

"Where are you?" yelled Tiger.

"I'm right here," said LC, bumping into Tiger. "Where's Gabby and Timothy?"

"We're over here where we left the horses," shouted Timothy.

LC and Tiger started walking. LC bumped into something and fell to the ground.

"Ow!" cried Gabby. "You just knocked me over."

"Sorry," said LC, helping her up.

"Where are the horses?" asked Tiger.

"We couldn't find them," said Timothy. "We'll have to go on foot."

LC, Gabby, Tiger, and Timothy walked and walked through the swirling dust. They got dirt in their eyes, up their noses, in their mouths, and even in their ears.

Then the storm began to blow more fiercely. A huge tumbleweed came crashing right into them.

"Aaahhh!" they all screamed

and fell to the ground. The tumbleweed rolled over them.

They got up and continued walking.

"Do you think we're going the right way?" Gabby asked.

Before anybody could answer, the dust cleared and they found themselves on a trail they'd never seen before. Behind them dust was still flying, but on the trail and beyond there was no storm at all.

"How weird," said Gabby, looking around.

"Actually, I think most dust storms are like that," said Timothy.

"I wonder where we are," said LC.

"And where the horses are," added Tiger.

Suddenly they heard the sound of hooves. A few seconds later Missy appeared on her horse, with the other horses right behind her.

"Am I glad to see you," said Gabby. "We got lost in the storm. How'd you find us?"

"I heard you scream," Missy said. "Otherwise I never would have found you at all. Hey, you know what?" she said, jumping down off her horse. "I think this is the Lost Trail of Ghost Valley."

"Whaddya mean?" asked Gabby.

"A long time ago there were some really bad rock slides around here," explained Missy. "A couple of cowboys got trapped under the rocks and died. So nobody ever comes this way anymore."

"Hmmm," said Timothy, staring at the ground. "If nobody ever comes here, then why are there tire tracks in the dirt right over there?" He pointed to the strip of dirt behind LC.

"Search me," said Missy.

LC bent down and stared at the tracks. There were a series of deep grooves with strange indentations between them.

"And what made those hoofprints?" asked Gabby. She pointed to a bunch of hoofprints next to the tire tracks.

"Those are cow prints for sure," said Missy.

"Hey," said LC. "What's that over there?"

He pointed to a circle of stones behind Missy.

"Looks like somebody made a fire," said Missy.

They all walked over to the stones. Imprinted in the dirt was a strange symbol in the shape of an upside-down Y in a circle.

"Do you think it's some kind of

message?" asked LC.

"Correct me if I'm wrong, Missy," said Timothy. "But I believe that symbol is most likely a brand. And it's very similar to your brand, which is a small upside-down V in a circle."

"That's true," said Missy.

"What's a brand?" asked LC.

"Every rancher has a certain symbol that is his brand," said Timothy. "And he brands all of his cattle with it so that if any of them get lost, whoever finds them will know who they belong to."

"So what does a brand have to do with anything?" asked Gabby.

"See that plank of wood over there," said Timothy, pointing to a long board leaning against a tree. "I believe that the cattle thief brings the stolen cows here to the Lost Trail, brands them with his brand so that they appear to belong to him, and then loads them into his truck."

"Who would do something like that?" asked LC.

"I don't know," said Missy. "But whoever it is has stolen all of our most valuable cows—except for one."

"Don't worry, Missy," said Gabby. "We'll get to the bottom of this."

"How are we going to do that?" asked Tiger.

"We'll come back here tonight for a stakeout," said Gabby. "That way we can catch the thief in the act."

"A stakeout?" said LC. "Are you sure that's a good idea?"

"Yep," said Gabby. "It's the only way."

CHAPTER 5

THE STAKEOUT

Late that night Gabby slipped out of her sleeping bag. "*Psst!* LC, wake up," she whispered. "It's time for the stakeout."

"What?" said LC.

"Take off those headphones," said Gabby. "Let's go."

LC climbed out of his sleeping bag. He put his headphones around his neck and clipped his Walkman to his belt. Then he woke up Gator, Tiger, and Timothy.

Gabby woke up Missy and the other girls.

"Who's got a flashlight?" asked Gator.

"I do," said Timothy. "I'll lead the way."

Everybody tiptoed past Mr. Hogwash, who was sound asleep, snoring loudly.

"Don't wake up Slim," said Gabby as they walked slowly past his sleeping bag.

The Critter Kids crept through the underbrush toward the Ghost Valley corral with only the light of one flashlight. It was very dark away from the campfire. Gator stumbled into Tiger, who stumbled into Henrietta, who fell against Su Su.

"Hey, watch where you're going!" Su Su said loudly.

"Shhhhh!" whispered Gabby.

Suddenly a low moaning sound pierced the air. *"Ooooow-ooooowwww!"* the voice cried. *"Ooooow-ooooow-ooooow!"* it came again from somewhere far off in the distance.

Everybody froze. A shiver ran up and down LC's spine.

"What was that?" whispered Velvet, hiding behind Tiger and Gator.

"Whatever it is, it's coming from the direction of Ghost Valley," said Timothy.

"It's the ghost," said Su Su.

"There's no such thing as ghosts," said Gabby. "Right?"

"Right," said LC, trying to sound brave.

The Critter Kids followed the sounds past Ghost Valley corral. "I think we're almost at the Lost Trail," said Missy.

Up ahead they saw an eerie light. It was coming from the clearing where they'd found the tire tracks and hoofprints. They crept closer and hid behind some bushes.

In the dim light they could just make out a figure moving around. They could also see the source of the loud moans. It was a cow. It had a rope around its neck and the figure was dragging it toward a truck.

"Hey," whispered Gabby. "Somebody's stealing a cow."

"Yeah," said LC. "They're loading it onto a truck."

"That looks like Duchess," said Missy. "She's the last of our valuable cows."

The figure dragged the cow up a board into the truck. Then he threw the board into the back of the truck.

"That must be the board we saw this

afternoon," said Gabby.

Then the figure threw a long metal pole into the back of the truck.

"That must be the branding iron," said Timothy.

"Now what?" asked Tiger.

"We better go back to the campsite," said Gabby. "We've got to tell Slim what's going on."

The Critter Kids hurried back toward the campsite. As soon as they got there, they ran over to Slim's sleeping bag.

"Who's gonna wake him up?" asked LC.

"I will," said Gabby. "Slim, Slim," she said, shaking Slim's sleeping bag. Slim didn't move.

"He must be a really deep sleeper," said Gator.

"Slim, Slim," said Gabby, shaking Slim's sleeping bag again.

Slim still didn't move. "Wait a minute," said LC. He reached down to pull back the sleeping bag. Suddenly a Red Hot Chili Critters song began to play. Everybody jumped.

"Sorry about that," LC said, pressing a button on his Walkman.

"There's nobody in the sleeping bag," said Tiger.

Everybody looked down. Slim wasn't there. The sleeping bag was stuffed with clothes!

"Wait a minute," said Gabby. "Where's Slim? What's going on here?"

Just then they heard something coming toward them. The Critter Kids and Missy all huddled together and stared in the direction of the sound. Out of the darkness Slim suddenly appeared and walked up to them.

"Howdy, partners," he said. "I was just takin' a little walk around makin' sure everything's A-OK. "

"Sure," said Gabby. "A little walk right on over to Ghost Valley corral and the Lost Trail to steal another cow."

"What are you talkin' about?" asked Slim.

"We saw you steal that cow," said LC. "And you're not gonna get away with it."

"Yeah!" everybody yelled.

Slim just laughed. "So what if I took the cows," he said. "You ain't got no proof. All you are is a bunch of kids. And nobody is gonna take your word over mine. So if

you'll excuse me, I'd like to get some shut-eye. We got a long ride back to the ranch in the mornin'."

"We're not just a bunch of kids!" shouted Gabby. "We're the Critter Kids and we're gonna get you!"

CHAPTER 6

BRANDED

The next morning everybody rode back to the ranch.

"What are we gonna do?" asked LC.

"You'll see," said Gabby. "Follow me."

Missy and the Critter Kids headed over to the mess hall. When they got there, everybody was already seated around the table, including Sheriff Buckeye and Deputy Doodle. They were all eating breakfast.

"I'm so hungry I could eat a horse," said Henrietta with a grin. "Just kidding."

The Critter Kids sat down. Gabby rapped her spoon against a water glass and stood up. "I'm glad to see you're all here. I have an important announcement to make," she said, looking around the table. "We know who's been stealing Mr. Big Horn's cattle."

"You do?" said Mr. Big Horn.

"Yes," said Gabby. "After a major investigation by myself and the Critter Kids Detective Club, along with some invaluable assistance from Missy, the cattle

thief's identity has been revealed and I think you should be aware that the thief is sitting at this very table."

Everyone gasped and looked around the table.

"Excuse me, young lady," said Sheriff Buckeye. "Would you tell us just who you are accusing of this crime?"

"Yes," said Gabby. "But first I would like to lay out the details of the case in order for you to better understand how we came to the conclusion that we did."

LC groaned. He wondered if Gabby would ever get to the point.

"Yesterday LC, Missy, Tiger, Timothy, and myself were on the Lost Trail," continued Gabby. "And there we discovered cattle hoofprints, tire tracks, and the mark of a branding iron imprinted in the dirt next to a ring of stones where a fire had been made."

"May I ask what all of this ... er ... hogwash ... has to do with anything?" asked Sheriff Buckeye.

"That's what I'm getting to," said Gabby. "Late that night under the cover of darkness the Critter Kids Detective Club staked out the area. And we witnessed the thief stealing Duchess, Mr. Big Horn's last prize heifer."

"Oh, no!" cried Mr. Big Horn. "Not Duchess."

"Lordy be, child," said Sheriff Buckeye. "Please don't hold us in suspense any longer."

"The thief, ladies and gentlemen, is Slim!" said Gabby. "In his truck you'll find the wooden board he used to load the cow onto the truck and the branding iron he used to change Mr. Big Horn's brand. And you'll also find that his tire tracks exactly match the tracks on the Lost Trail."

Slim chuckled. "Sorry to disappoint you kids," he said. "Sheriff, you *will* find a brandin' iron in my truck and you *will* find a wooden board 'cause that's exactly what *I* found last night when *I* went out investigatin'."

"Yeah, but what about your tire prints on the trail?" asked Tiger.

"Yeah," said Henrietta, popping a corn muffin in her mouth.

"Aw, shucks," said Slim. "Everybody 'round here drives pickup trucks."

"Gabby," began Mr. Hogwash in his sternest voice, "you should never accuse someone of a crime unless you can prove their guilt beyond the shadow of a doubt."

Gabby sank down in her seat.

"We tried," said LC.

He leaned across the table to grab the pitcher of orange juice. By accident, he hit the PLAY button on his Walkman. Suddenly he heard Slim's voice coming out of the headphones that were around his neck.

"Not so fast, Slim," said LC, jumping up. "I've got proof." LC put his Walkman on the table and unplugged the headphones. He pressed the PLAY button again: "So what if I took the cows. You ain't got no proof. All you are is a bunch of kids. And nobody is gonna take your word over mine . . ."

Everyone gasped!

"Well, Slim, it looks like these kids have nailed you," said Sheriff Buckeye.

"Why'd you do it, Slim?" asked Mr. Big Horn.

Slim hung his head. "I did it for the money," said Slim.

"But what about those hoofprints in the Ghost Valley corral?" asked Deputy Doodle.

"Shut up, Doodle!" said Sheriff Buckeye. "Forget those prints. We done caught us the thief and that's all that matters."

"Aw, shucks," said Deputy Doodle. "I still think that ghost had something to do with this."

Sheriff Buckeye and Deputy Doodle led Slim outside to the patrol car.

"I don't know how I can thank you kids enough," said Mr. Big Horn.

"Nice goin', dude," said Tiger to LC.

"Yeah," said Missy with a big smile. "You saved the ranch."

The next day the Critter Kids packed their things. They brought everything out to the bus, where Missy and Mr. Big Horn were standing.

"You're all welcome at Big Horn Ranch anytime," said Mr. Big Horn, patting LC on the back so hard he almost fell. "Sheriff Buckeye found the guy Slim sold my cattle to and got 'em all back."

The Critter Kids cheered.

As Gabby got onto the bus, she turned to Missy. "You can be our special agent in the West," she said. "So if anything suspicious happens, just let us know."

"Will do," said Missy.

LC shook his head and started to get on the bus.

"I have something for you," said Missy.

"Me?" said LC.

"Yeah," said Missy. She handed LC a rope. "This is my lucky lasso. I want you to have it. It's for tough guys just like you."

"Thanks," said LC with a big smile.

Two weeks later LC and the Critter Kids received a telegram from Missy. Mr. Hogwash read it out loud to the class:

TELEGRAM TO: THE CRITTER KIDS DETECTIVE CLUB. STOP.

FROM: SPECIAL AGENT IN THE WEST. STOP.

THE DISAPPEARING HOOFPRINTS HAVE SUDDENLY APPEARED AGAIN IN GHOST VALLEY. STOP. AND SLIM IS MILES AWAY BEHIND BARS. STOP. WHEN CAN YOU GET HERE? STOP.

Oh, no, thought LC, not again . . .